our Telephone Renewals 020 8489

HARINGEY LIBRARIES

OK MUST BE RETURNED ON OR B

E LAST DATE MARKED BELO

MARCUS GARVEY

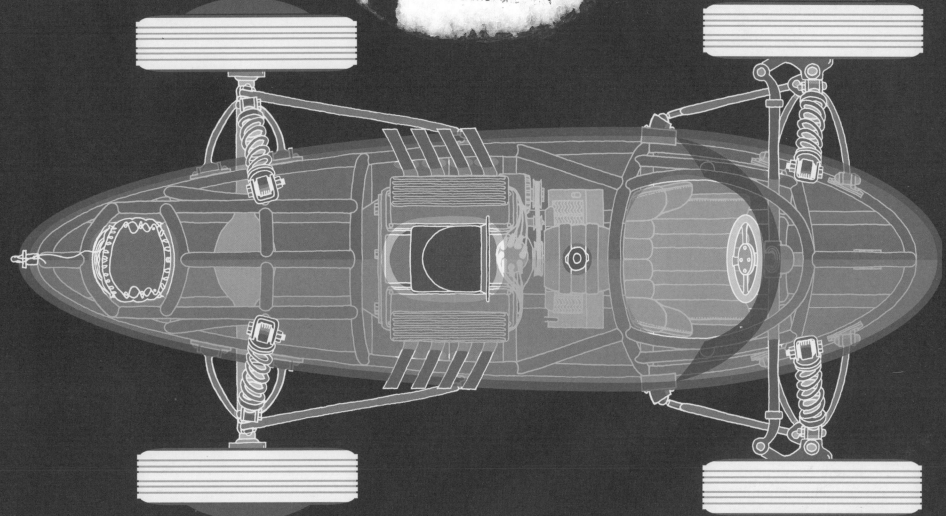

70003009110 5

HARINGEY PUBLIC LIBRARY	
70003009110 5	
PETERS	05-Mar-2019
£14.99	

SPEED BIRDS

ALAN SNOW

To Bobby, Pete, Darin, Dave, Frank, Sue, Steph, Cathy, and Finn –
whose work/life balance is adjusted with a spanner

OXFORD
UNIVERSITY PRESS

Great Clarendon Street, Oxford OX2 6DP
Oxford University Press is a department of the University of Oxford.
It furthers the University's objective of excellence in research, scholarship,
and education by publishing worldwide. Oxford is a registered trade mark of
Oxford University Press in the UK and in certain other countries

Text and illustrations copyright © Alan Snow 2018
The moral rights of the author and illustrator have been asserted
Database right Oxford University Press (maker)
First published 2018
All rights reserved. No part of this publication may be reproduced,
stored in a retrieval system, or transmitted, in any form or by any means,
without the prior permission in writing of Oxford University Press,
or as expressly permitted by law, or under terms agreed with the appropriate
reprographics rights organization. Enquiries concerning reproduction
outside the scope of the above should be sent to the Rights Department,

Oxford University Press, at the address above
You must not circulate this book in any other binding or cover
and you must impose this same condition on any acquirer

British Library Cataloguing in Publication Data

Data available
ISBN: 978-0-19-275872-9 (hardback)

1 3 5 7 9 10 8 6 4 2

Printed in China

Paper used in the production of this book is a natural,
recyclable product made from wood grown in sustainable forests.
The manufacturing process conforms to the environmental
regulations of the country of origin.

SPEED BIRDS

ALAN SNOW

OXFORD
UNIVERSITY PRESS

On a hill in a wood, there lived some crows. One spring, a chick hatched who was smaller than the rest, with white feathers in his tail and a glint of curiosity in his eye. As his mother fed him and cared for him, she talked to him of the **WONDERS** of the world.

'There are many things to discover in the world,' she said. 'If you stay curious, use your mind, and believe in yourself, there is no limit to what you can achieve out there.'

'But you must be careful, too,' she continued. 'There are falcons about, and they can be **DEADLY** to crows. They can fly at **242 MILES PER HOUR**—faster than any other bird. If you see one, stay out of its way.'

But one day when the young crows were hunting insects, the smallest bird spotted a scarecrow. As he flew away from the group to investigate this strange figure, he didn't notice a TINY DOT appear high overhead in the sky. He didn't notice as the dot grew LARGER and CLOSER as it *plummeted* towards him. It was only when a shadow flickered across the scarecrow that the small bird looked up to see a falcon *diving*, its wings held back and its talons outstretched. Just in time, the small crow *darted* underneath the scarecrow's arm. There was a SQUAWK and the falcon was gone.

The small bird should have been terrified, but instead he was entranced by the speed of the falcon. 'Flying that fast must be the best feeling ever. I'd give anything to be the fastest bird in the world!'

Soon it was autumn and the crows' leader called them together. 'Winter is coming and there are just too many of us crows for the wood to support. It's time for the young and adventurous to set out into the world and build a life elsewhere.'

Some young crows were a little nervous about leaving, but the small bird couldn't wait to set out on his own voyage of DISCOVERY.

'Remember,' his mother told him, 'if you stay curious, use your mind, and believe in yourself, there is no limit to what you can achieve.'

The next morning, after a hearty breakfast of nuts, berries, and worms, the young crows set off. They flew south, because they knew their first winter would be more comfortable there. As they flew they cawed to each other about what kind of home they should look for. They spotted other woods but the small bird urged them on. 'Let's keep going—I know there are **WONDERS** out there for us to discover.'

As the days passed, the land slowly changed from farmland and woodland, to rocky mountains and deserts, and the air grew warmer.

One evening, when the crows were longing for rest, they spied an old tree on the horizon.

'Let's roost here,' said one of the birds. 'This lone tree won't make much of a home, so we'll have to fly on again tomorrow—but at least we'll be safe tonight.'

The small crow said nothing. There was something very interesting about that tree. It was too dark to see properly now—but in the morning he would be able to investigate.

The next morning, the small crow awoke and could hardly believe his eyes. Stretching before him was a magnificent salt lake, and lodged in the branches of the tree was a rusty old car. Directly below was a yard containing yet more old cars and machinery. *Just wait until the others see this*, he thought—and then cawed loudly to wake them all up.

To their **DELIGHT**, the young crows discovered bugs and beetles to eat in every shadow of the yard. One crow found a tap that dripped into a barrel, and they took turns drinking and refreshing themselves after their long journey.

Once he had eaten and drunk his fill, the small bird looked around in **WONDER** at the scrap and wrecks around them. There was so much to investigate. Hopping around **EXCITEDLY**, he spotted a shed with a broken window, and **FLAPPED** over to explore.

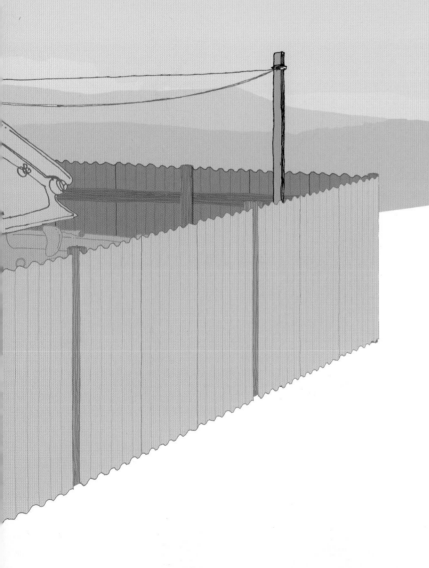

Inside, the shed was a den of **WONDERS** such as the small crow had never dreamed of. He called the other birds over and one by one they hopped inside. The shed was filled with tools, machines, car parts, and there were large drawings of a type of car the crows had never seen before.

One crow pointed to some cups, trophies, and photographs on a shelf above the drawing board. 'These are speed trophies!' said the small crow with excitement. **'SOMEONE WAS USING THESE CARS TO GO FAST!'**

Exploring further, the crows found a set of plans and a notebook packed with drawings and lists.

'What do they all mean?' asked one of the crows.

The small crow smiled as he studied the diagrams carefully. 'They tell us everything we need to know to build one of these cars,' he said. 'If we just follow the instructions, we can go faster than we ever dreamed of. **Faster** than any crow has ever travelled before. **Faster** even than a falcon.'

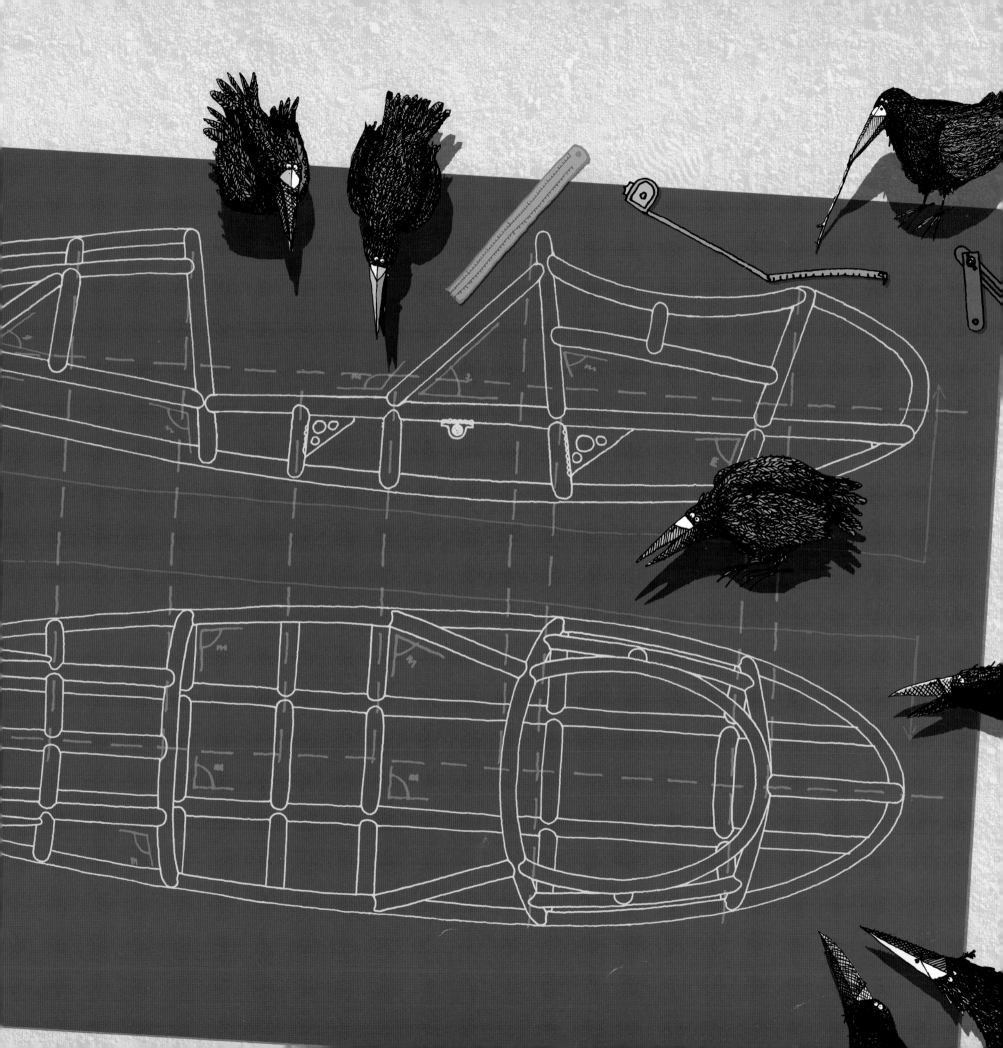

Enthused by the small crow's passion for speed, the young birds set to work to find all the parts listed in the notebook. None of them could believe how many parts went into making a car.

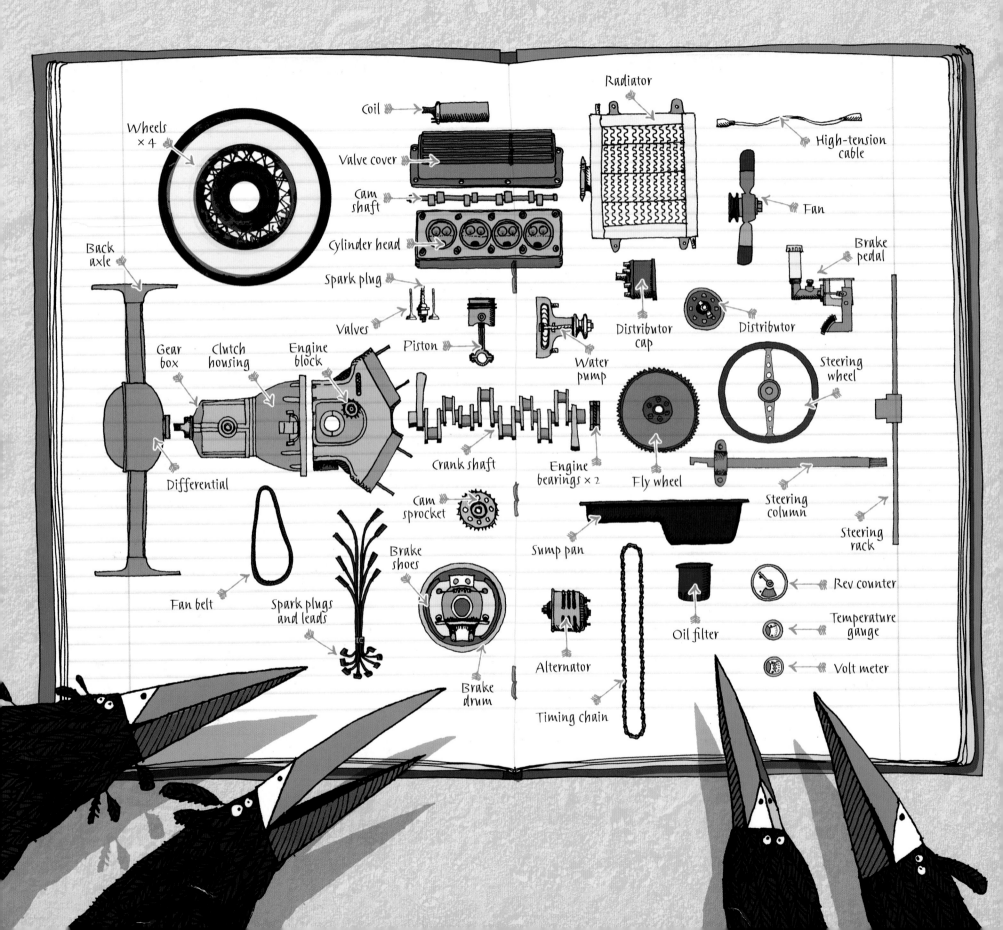

Rummaging around in scrapheaps and under piles of rusting metal, it only took a few hours to find all the parts, including the body of the car, which they discovered was made from an old fuel tank from an aeroplane, called a belly tank.

'That was easy,' said one of the crows. 'We will have this car built in no time at all!'

The small crow, studying the notebook carefully, shook his head. 'If we want this car to go *fast*, we have to do it right. We need to clean, polish, and oil all the parts. Everything must be PERFECT.'

The crows soon found out that 'doing it right' was a lengthy business. It took them a long time to get all the parts ready for assembly.

Whenever the crows flagged, the small crow kept them going, finding the next steps in the notebook and urging them on. And whenever any of the birds tried to sneak into a shady corner to eat bugs, the small crow sought them out and reminded them of the excitement of **speed** and of how THRILLING it would be to travel *faster* than a falcon.

As the days passed by and turned into weeks, the crows learned to bend and cut metal tubes, to clamp and saw, and to weld metal parts together with a machine that produced SPARKS OF ELECTRICITY to heat the metal. One of the crows was appointed as health-and-safety officer, and insisted that the welder crows wore goggles to protect their eyes from the sparks.

When the frame of the car was finally assembled, and all the other parts were **GLEAMING** and ready to be put together, the crows felt a huge sense of achievement. Perhaps they could really do this!

'Now it's time for us to build the engine,' said the small crow, who had spent many hours studying the diagrams and instructions in the notebook. 'It should be quite simple. As long as we understand the principles I don't think we can go wrong.

'Engines mix air and fuel, and spray it into a container, then set it alight.

'The mixture **EXPLODES** and pushes a piston down a barrel, which in turn makes a crank go round.

'When the crank goes round it returns the piston up the barrel, pushes the burnt gases out of the engine, and then sucks in more air and fuel so it can all happen again.'

When he finished speaking, the small crow became aware that the other crows were gazing at him with puzzled eyes and open beaks. 'Er . . . simple?' one of them stuttered.

The small crow smiled. 'Just trust me,' he said. 'Together we can do this. Let's go over it again . . .'

HOW ENGINES WORK

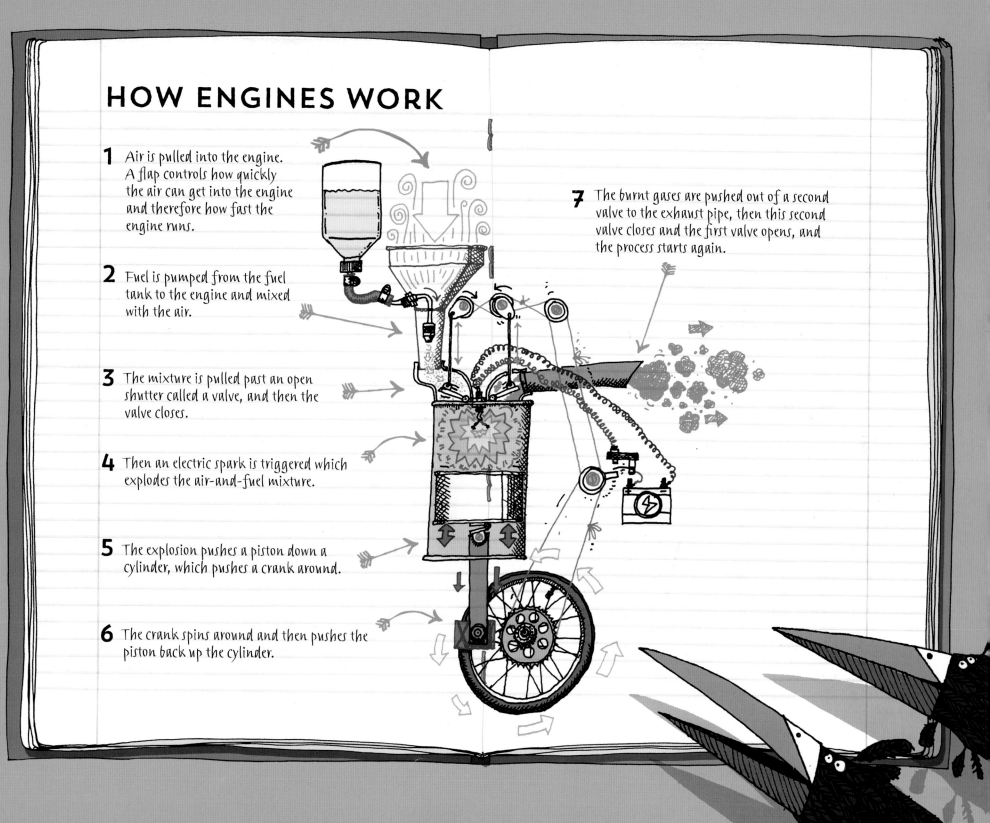

1 Air is pulled into the engine. A flap controls how quickly the air can get into the engine and therefore how fast the engine runs.

2 Fuel is pumped from the fuel tank to the engine and mixed with the air.

3 The mixture is pulled past an open shutter called a valve, and then the valve closes.

4 Then an electric spark is triggered which explodes the air-and-fuel mixture.

5 The explosion pushes a piston down a cylinder, which pushes a crank around.

6 The crank spins around and then pushes the piston back up the cylinder.

7 The burnt gases are pushed out of a second valve to the exhaust pipe, then this second valve closes and the first valve opens, and the process starts again.

Once the crows understood how the engine should work, it was time to build it from the parts they had prepared. To give them the power they needed to go fast, they were going to construct the engine with eight pistons.

Using spanners, gauges, screwdrivers, and sockets, the crows bolted the big engine block onto a stand so it was steady and level, and started to add the parts. It was like a jigsaw and took a long time as everything had to be done in exactly the correct order, and nothing could be missed out.

The small crow made sure that he studied the plans in the notebook carefully as they put the pieces together. From time to time he would stop the others and make them reposition a part more carefully.

'I think we'll need to move those spark plugs as they haven't got quite the right amount of space around them—look at the measurements on the gauge. If we don't get it right, the spark won't be able to IGNITE the fuel in the cylinders, and the engine won't work.'

The crows worked long and hard. Building the engine was careful work, but they knew it had to be perfect if they wanted the engine to run as fast as possible.

'Remember, we need this car to go fast . . . ***faster than a falcon*** . . .'

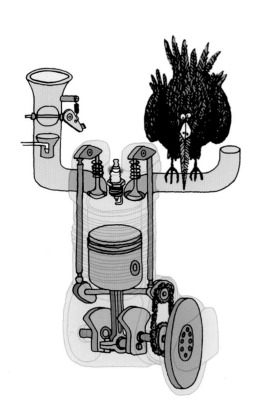

At the start of the next day, the small crow gathered all the birds together. The crows were all tired after the weeks of work, but they could tell that the small bird had something important to say.

'TODAY IS THE DAY!' he said excitedly.
'TODAY WE WILL FINISH OUR CAR!'

The birds cawed with DELIGHT. Could the end really be in sight at last?

The small crow split the birds into two teams. The first team put together the working parts of the car, which included the wheels, springs, brakes, and steering. Then it was time to fit the engine.

They used chains and the junkyard crane to raise the engine, then rolled the car frame under it, and lowered the engine into place very carefully. Then they had to fit all the other parts, including the electrics, the fan to cool the engine, the water pump, the radiator, and pipes.

The second group worked on the outer bodywork of the car. They cut holes in the belly tank to allow space for the wheels, the air cylinders that cooled the engine, the exhaust pipes, and a cockpit for the crows. Then it needed a paint job!

Once the paint was dry, the seat and steering wheel were bolted in, and finally the two halves of the belly tank were fixed over the frame. The crows had a car!

The birds gathered around the car and stared in WONDERMENT. They decided that the car deserved a name and called it . . . 'SPEED BIRD.'

'Now I'm going to show you how we should time our speed-record attempt,' said the small bird. 'We have to measure out a straight mile on the salt lake, with a long tape, and then time how many seconds it takes to drive the course. If we divide the number of seconds in an hour, which is 3600 seconds, by the seconds it takes to drive the mile, that will tell us the speed of the car in miles per hour.'

'Enough of all that,' cawed another bird, looking at the little crow. 'Can't we just start it up and go?'

The little crow smiled. 'This is no ordinary car,' he said. 'Most cars have a battery-powered motor to start the engine. We'll need to get this one going a different way. Are you all ready for one more job?'

The little crow explained that to drive the car, they would need to use the motion of the wheels to start the engine. 'We need to tow the car to get it started,' he said.

Weary, but **EXCITED**, the crows put on their helmets, which were made from tennis balls they had found in the yard, and left the small crow alone in the cockpit. Then they used ropes to tow the car out of the yard and onto the salt lake.

The **SPEED BIRD** reached its top speed just before it passed a bird on the starter post, who **WAVED** a flag to tell a second crow at the end of the mile track to start a stop-watch.

As the car picked up speed, the engine gave a loud **COUGH** and **SPARKED** into life. Quickly the birds released the ropes and dropped one by one into the car with the small bird. The small bird slowly opened up the throttle to let more fuel and air into the engine, and the car began to gain speed.

The crows drove the car backwards and forwards across the salt lake to warm up the engine. Eventually, the little crow said, 'I think it's time to find out how fast this car can really go. It's time for a *speed* attempt!'

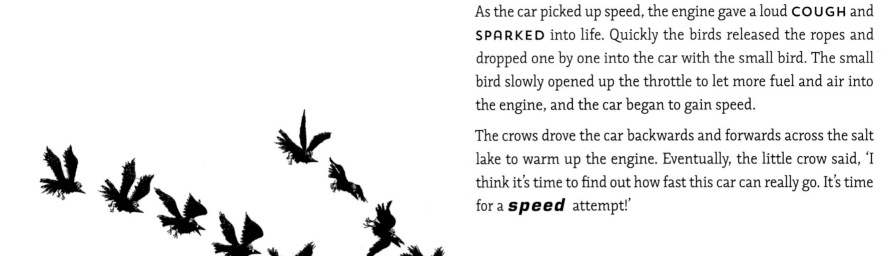

In what seemed like only a few seconds the car *rushed* past the timer bird, who stopped the watch again.

The small bird pressed the brake pedal and released a parachute from the back of the car to slow it down. The car eventually came to a stop and the crows felt stunned as they **FLAPPED** out of the cockpit.

'WOW!' they cawed. 'I CAN'T BELIEVE IT REALLY WORKED!'

But the small bird didn't say anything. He went straight to the timer bird to look at the stop-watch. Had they done it?

He looked at the watch quietly for a while as he calculated the speed. '15.79 seconds' said the watch. That meant their speed had been **228 MILES PER HOUR**. It was ***very, very fast***. But not fast enough.

The small crow felt downcast. He had made the others work so hard—and for nothing. They had not achieved their goal. They had not gone as fast as a falcon. He couldn't do it after all.

'Let's just go back to our roost,' he said quietly.

The small crow moped around for a week. The other crows tried to cheer him up, but he just sat in his roost with no interest in anything. 'I've let you all down,' he said sadly.

The other crows were worried. They felt so proud that they had built a car—they might not be the fastest birds in the world, but they were surely the best mechanics! They wanted the small crow to feel happy, too.

'Remember what he always says to us,' they told each other. 'Stay curious, use your mind, and believe in yourself. Let's try to find a way to work this out.'

After some discussion, the crows had the idea of looking in the notebook. Sure enough, they were excited to find a page headed: 'Ways to make your car go **_faster_**'.

'Let's take this to the small crow!'

WAYS TO MAKE YOUR CAR GO FASTER

1. 'LOWER WEIGHT'

Lighten the car by removing anything that isn't necessary… and that means EVERYTHING that isn't necessary.

2. 'INCREASE POWER'

A bigger engine will provide more power. Search the other trucks and cars. Getting as much fuel and air into an engine as quickly as possible will give it even more power.

3. 'REDUCE FRICTION'

When a car moves it experiences a force, called friction, which slows it down. Check that the airflow over the car is good. When a car goes really fast, the air is almost like a wall it has to push against. Cover the wheels and make a windshield for the cockpit to help the air flow more easily around the car. All the moving parts in the car also experience friction, so make sure every moving part is oiled and greased to help it move.

This new information was just what the small crow needed to give him back his enthusiasm. 'We'll try all three!' he said.

First, the crows worked on making the car **LIGHTER**. They took out the seat and cut all the pipes around the engine so they were just long enough to do their jobs.

'And only the lightest crow should ride in the car this time,' cawed one of the bigger crows. He looked at the small crow. 'We all believe in you. Please will you drive the car for us all?'

The small crow looked at his friends and smiled. 'Of course, I will.'

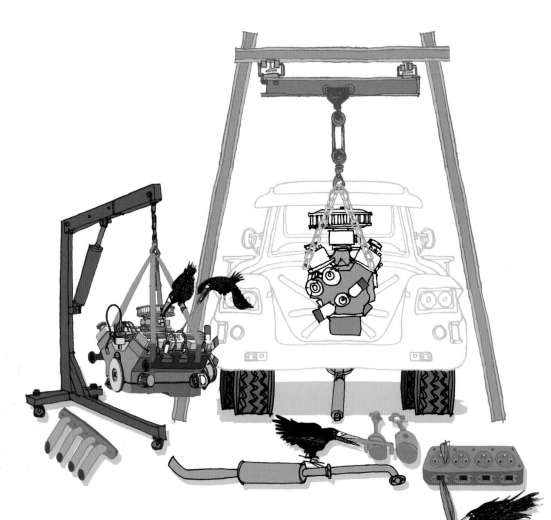

Next, to give the car more **POWER**, the birds took a bigger engine from a truck. The engine was a similar type to their previous engine, which meant they could fit parts from their old engine onto it, and the new engine would fit easily into their car.

'That should make the car much faster,' said the small crow. 'But before we drive again, we need to try to improve the friction, too. Let's work out if there is anything we do to help the air slide more smoothly over the car.'

In a corner of the yard was a massive fan fixed to an electric motor. The crows rolled the car in front of the fan, put the brakes on, and turned on the wind. Then the small crow held up a pipe with that was connected to a tin can containing a smouldering rag.

Smooth trails of smoke ran out of the pipe and over the car. Instantly they could see where air was getting caught up. Around the wheels the smoke **PUFFED** and **SWIRLED** in a messy cloud, and the same seemed to be happening over the cockpit.

The crows made a small windscreen and fitted it along with wheel covers, but just before they were done the eager crow who was operating the fan turned it back on again. The sudden **BLAST** of air caught the working crows by surprise and took off quite a few of their feathers.

'STOP!'

screamed the birds in front of the fan, as their feathers were blown off.

'YOU'RE GOING TO MAKE US BALD!'

The fan slowed and a very guilty-looking bird at the controls apologized.

'You *should* be sorry!' complained a crow. 'You know that if we lose feathers we can't fly as fast.'

The small crow looked at the lost feathers that were now settling all over the yard. They gave him a fantastic idea.

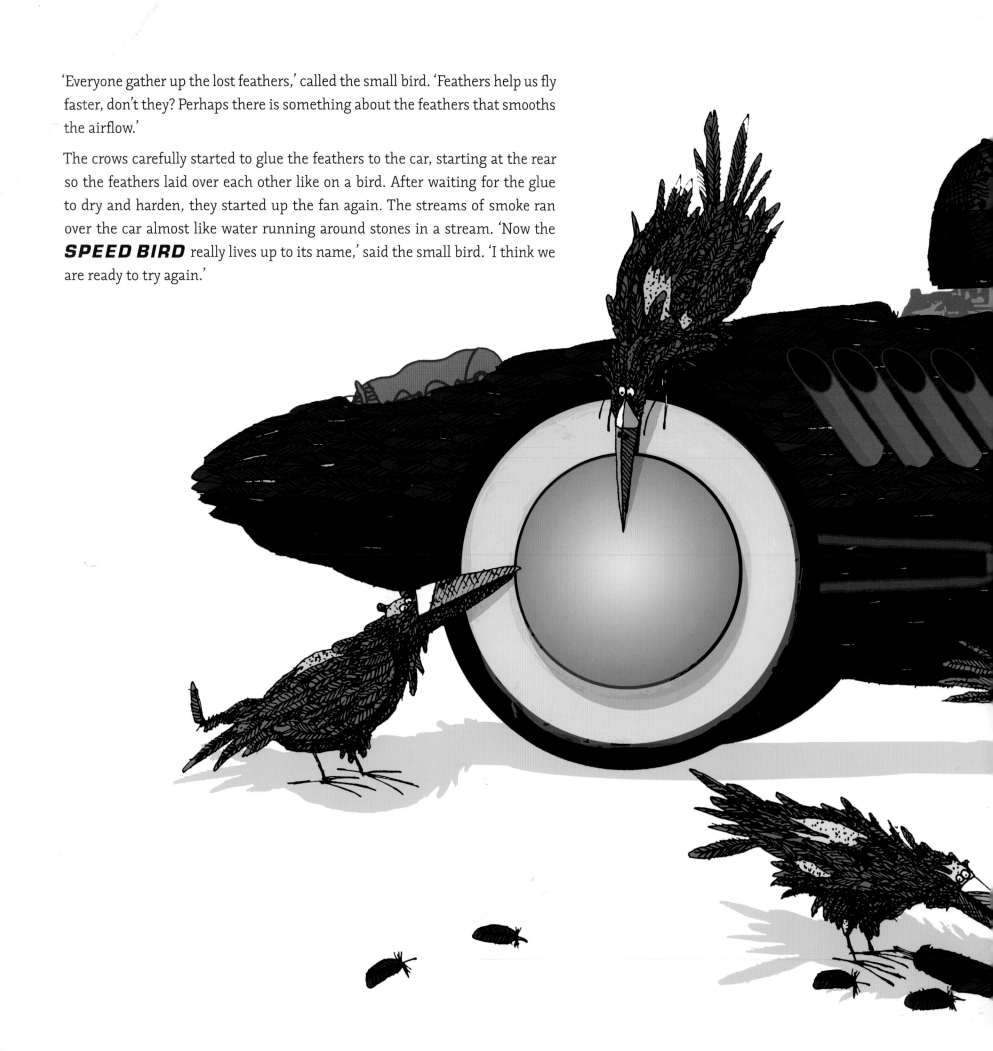

'Everyone gather up the lost feathers,' called the small bird. 'Feathers help us fly faster, don't they? Perhaps there is something about the feathers that smooths the airflow.'

The crows carefully started to glue the feathers to the car, starting at the rear so the feathers laid over each other like on a bird. After waiting for the glue to dry and harden, they started up the fan again. The streams of smoke ran over the car almost like water running around stones in a stream. 'Now the **SPEED BIRD** really lives up to its name,' said the small bird. 'I think we are ready to try again.'

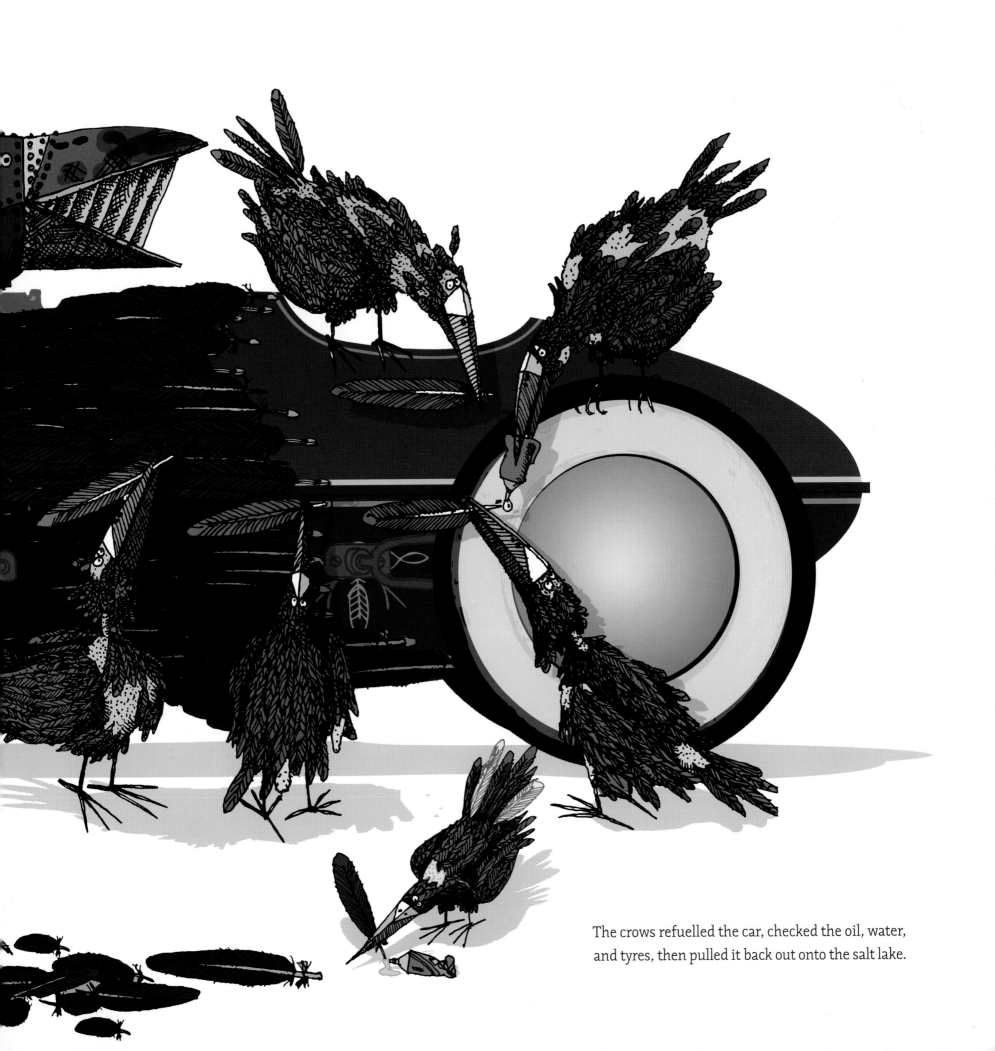

The crows refuelled the car, checked the oil, water, and tyres, then pulled it back out onto the salt lake.

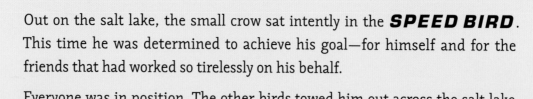

Out on the salt lake, the small crow sat intently in the **SPEED BIRD**. This time he was determined to achieve his goal—for himself and for the friends that had worked so tirelessly on his behalf.

Everyone was in position. The other birds towed him out across the salt lake, **FLAPPING** their wings in unison. As the car picked up speed, the small bird's heart **POUNDED** as the engine **ROARED** and the other crows fell away. He stared straight in front of him, totally focused on the flags ahead.

As the wind **whooshed** over the windscreen and past his head, he pictured the falcon once again in his mind, **swooping** with that dizzying, magnificent speed.

'We crows stayed curious . . .' he said to himself. 'We used our minds . . . The others believed in me—and now—I need to believe in myself.'

As the car hit top speed and roared past the starter post, the small bird who wanted to be the fastest bird in the world gripped the steering wheel, gritted his beak . . . and believed.

The crows held their breath as the **SPEED BIRD** started to shimmer in the hot air over the salt lake. The crows could feel the ground starting to rumble as the car passed the first cones and the timer bird started the watch.

'**GO ON!**' the crows all cawed at the top of their voices.

The car thundered past the crows, shaking them with a blast of hot air as it went. The timer crow hit the stop-watch button the very moment the car passed the second cones.

The crows watched the car slow down and make its way back across the salt lake towards them. The engine cut, and the small crow tumbled out of the cockpit. 'Well, what time did we get?' he said.

'We haven't looked,' said the crow with the watch. 'We were waiting for you.'

Together the crows peered at the stop-watch. 'We completed the mile in 14.81 seconds,' said one. 'We went faster than before. But is it fast enough to beat the record?' said another. 'I wish I had some fingers to count on.'

While the other birds tried to work out whether they had broken the record, the small bird spoke up. 'Do you know what that time means, everyone?'

'CROWS ARE OFFICIALLY THE FASTEST BIRDS IN THE WORLD!'

To their **DELIGHT**, the young crows had reached a top speed of **243 MILES PER HOUR**—making them faster than the falcon . . . just!

The crows celebrated by **SINGING** loudly (if the cawing of crows could ever be described as singing) and **DANCING** across the salt lake.

Then, as the party began to wind down . . .

'I guess we're world-record holders now,' said a crow. 'Just like the Rüppell's vulture.'

'They can fly at over thirty-thousand feet,' said another. 'They're the HIGHEST-FLYING BIRDS IN THE WORLD ...'

'Wow, that is incredible,' said the small crow. 'Flying that high must be the best feeling ever. I'd give anything to be the highest-flying bird in the world.'

And all the other crows looked at each other and smiled.

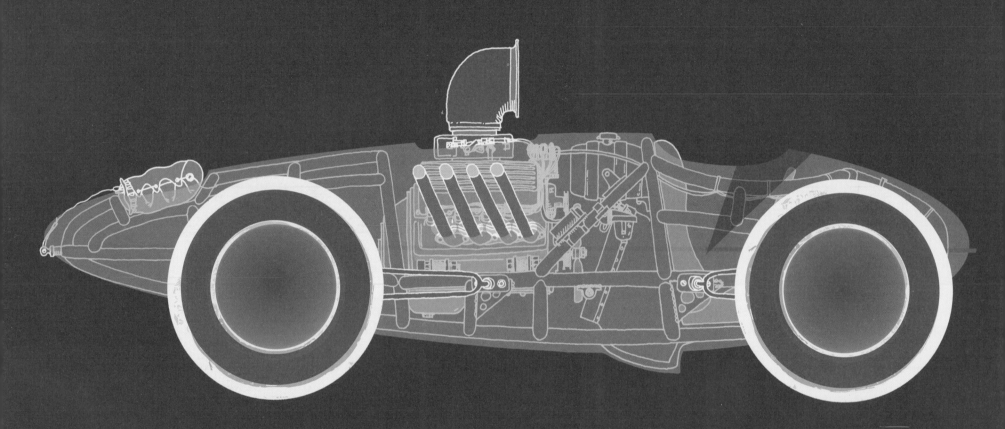